Of The Sea

Of The Sea

G.C. Bailey

G.C. Bailey

November 2020

Cover by Devotion/Shutterstock.com

Photography by Southern Exposures Photography

southernexposuresinfo@yahoo.com

Printed in the United States of America

First Printing: November 2020

Kindle Direct Publishing

ISBN 979-8-597-93068-8

Contents

I have spent most of my life waiting for you to say those three words:
"I love you."

He was rugged, possessing a wild spirit-

and she loved him for it.

He looked into her eyes and suddenly knew
she had made a permanent home in his heart.

Of The Sea

She didn't realize he was what she

had been looking for all

along until it was too late.

G.C. Bailey

A Thousand Splendid Suns

Should I live a thousand years
To see a thousand splendid suns,
To have but a moment with you
I would surrender every one.

For every time I look upon you
It feels as though for the first time,
And anticipation wells within
With the longing to make you mine.

To rule as king of your heart
To have your mind, body, and soul,
To always have you by my side
To cherish when I am old

I want all your midnights
To hold you in the quiet places,
For only you can fill the void
Of my heart's empty spaces.

I've lived a life full of adventure
And I've enjoyed the days gone by,
Yet it all means nothing
Without you by my side

To have days without you,
I wouldn't keep a single one.
Not for a thousand lifetimes
Nor for a thousand splendid suns.

Of The Sea

She visited him every night in his dreams.

Every morning he wished

she would visit when he was awake.

My Favorite Things

Riding down dirt roads and late nights spent talking,
Attending music concerts and going clothes shopping,
Halloween parties and the sound of you laughing,
These are a few of my favorite things.

Summer night movies and early school mornings,
Mistake of My Life playing and the sound of you sighing,
Wondering what our future might bring,
These are a few of my favorite things.

Road trips and you in bright colored dresses,
4-wheeler riding and making mud messes,
Singing *Dilemma* so loudly with me,
These are a few of my favorite things.

When the world's gone
Stir crazy.
When I'm feeling sad.
I simply remember these favorite things,
And then I don't feel so bad.

Dozens of phone calls and all day spent texting,
You looking pretty and my heart melting,
All of the places that we got to see,
These are a few of my favorite things.

Watching *A Christmas Story* and tree decorating,
Time with my best friend and gentle hand holding,
Dreaming about what our life should be,

Of The Sea

These are a few of my favorite things.

When the world's gone
Stir crazy.
When I'm feeling sad.
I simply remember these favorite things,
And then I don't feel so bad.

Sitting beside you and being so cozy,
You laughing so hard you start nose snorting,
Times alone with you mean so much to me.
These are a few of my favorite things.

Being with you never makes me feel lonely,
I have loved you and loved you only,
Will you spend the rest of your life with me?
This would be my absolute favorite thing.

When the world's gone
Stir crazy.
When I'm feeling sad.
I simply remember these favorite things,
And then I don't feel so bad.

G.C. Bailey

He sensed her presence

even before his eyes found her.

9

It was the small details she noticed-

the way his lip would curl,

the way his nose twitched,

or the look in his eyes;

and she would know his thoughts.

She looked into his eyes
    and saw that she was truly loved.

Home is Where the Heart is

They say "Home is where the heart is."

That must be true.

For I am a lonely wanderer in this world,

Because my home, my heart, is with you.

Like a hunter, he studied her and knew
the places her soul would hide.

He delicately approached her

when she was most vulnerable,

and she knew he would never leave her side.

Of The Sea

He knew all her contradictions and intricacies

and loved her not in spite of them,

but because of them.

G.C. Bailey

He came to her side,

gently placing his arm around her,

                   And she was sure of him.

Fly fishermen use their rods like skilled painters, to create art on a canvas created by God.

Crying to the Moon

Tonight I was sitting and drinking beneath the stars,

Trying to forget all the pain and deep scars.

With the bottle in my hand I cried to the moon,

Asking it why I am still so in love with you.

The man in the moon looked down at my cries

And told me in a voice that was kind, as well as wise;

"That you hurt, this I know is true,

But don't you see the life she has breathed into you?"

I looked at the bottle and gave a sad sigh.

I sat down on the ground and continued to cry.

"Yes, but I'm so broken I wish to die."

The moon gave a smile, and this was his reply:

"Love such as this will endure through all time.

Love her selflessly- do not repine.

For thousands of years I have shone over this world,

And witnessed many a man in despair of a girl.

Of The Sea

Perhaps one day, she will come to love you too,

But if not, don't despair- continue to love her as you do."

With that, the moon's face faded and went dim.

There were so many questions I wished to ask of him.

I looked up now at what was simply just the moon.

Taking the bottle I thought, "It's the alcohol you buffoon."

Yet, now I felt different, as I sat there in the night.

I knew that everything would somehow be all right.

I love her; that will forever remain a fact,

But along with my words, I must also act.

So with resolution I have come by your side,

I love you with all of me-and will until I die.

A kiss on her forehead is all

that is required

to calm her fears.

Of The Sea

My heart is an inland soul at sea,

For it longs for that which was not meant to be.

A good woman is not
put off when a man
speaks to her from
his heart.

Leaving

I must be leaving soon,

But I will fight to come back to you.

But if upon foreign soil should I die,

And my body is left where it lies,

My soul will fly like a winged dove

Back to you and this homeland that I love.

And there it will rest upon that hallowed ground,

That you may feel my presence-

Even though I am no longer around.

I loved her fully and gave all of myself to her,

But in the end she broke my heart

And left me in scattered pieces.

She was the only one who had my heart…

my whole heart.

G.C. Bailey

His heart chose her,

but her heart never chose him.

How Will I Be Remembered

How will I be remembered,
When I, my final breath take?
For those I loved, did I their lives better make?
Would my friends and those who knew me best
Say I was a good man now laid to rest?

Will they remember that I lived and loved fully,
And will they sigh and say I will be missed truly?
Or will they say I was wretched all my lifetime
Cruel and selfish; never offering a poor man a dime?

Is this world better with me done and gone,
To be placed into the ground and missed by no one?
What have I done for my fellow man
That makes my pitiful life worth a damn?

Oh God! I pray forgive the terrible deeds I've done,
When on the fields of battle that the day be won.
Greatness always seemed right at the cusp,
Yet try as I might, my deeds were never enough.

Would my sins be forgiven if I made a final stand?
Or, has God abandoned me- then to hell I am damned.
Perhaps it's not too late! There is still time at hand
To love my fellow brother and be a better man!

God, grant me the strength to get through another day.
Use me to help those I meet travelling along the way.
Make me courageous, honorable, noble and true;
Set an example, that Your light may shine through.

To those I love: I beg thee forgive my shortfalls,
And remember me fondly, when it is time for the palls.

Of The Sea

When I dream, she is always with me;

I wish to never be awake.

But even my dreams are inadequate,

For her perfections and her imperfections

Are only the perfect projection of my imperfect memory.

Both of these:

Her and my memory of her,

Are too beautiful to be bound by dreams.

She had never known true love

until he showed her.

He loved her wildly and with an open heart-

as a woman should truly be loved.

She was his inspiration; his muse.
She was his life and his love true.

But when she smiles;

ah,

I get a glimpse of heaven.

The moment I realized I loved her,

I changed and became a man.

Whirlwind

You're a whirlwind in the figure of a woman
Born on an ocean breeze.
Overcome by the power of your beauty,
I watch you run wild and free.

You swept my heart
Like a whirlwind.
I fell apart
In the whirlwind.

You don't know what you do to me
Just by giving me a smile.
You started a fire in my heart
That drives me wild.

Like a whirlwind you pick me up
And you throw me down.
But every time you touch me
My heart leaps with a bound.

G.C. Bailey

Woman, why don't you realize

I've become a ramblin' man?

Tracing your footsteps everywhere I go

Without purpose and with no plan.

Like a whirlwind you stir my heart.

You know my words are true.

I just need a little of your time

To show how much I love you.

He wept, but he wasn't embarrassed.

She saw him and knew he wept for her-

and knew that he truly did love her.

I called her name and she heard
the longing in my throat.

We loved with a passion that

surpassed all understanding.

The Ascent of Stan

Pangs of silence from the room upstairs
Then cries fill the air
Friends separated and alone

All grieving that you're gone

I cried alone when I heard the news

I'm still unbelieving that it's true

I play it over and over in my head

All the things left unsaid

The ascent of Stan

You had so much living still at hand

Taken when still so young a man

Now you're one of God's guardians

I visit the places we used to love

Fly fishing and hunting dove

Of The Sea

How did this fit into God's plan

Nothing's the same without you Stan

Years have gone by but the pain remains

We went on living yet it's not the same

One day I'll pass over too

And will be in heaven with you

The ascent of Stan

God's new angel in heaven

Smile down when you can

I'll be smiling back at you Stan

When he first saw her,

his heart skipped a beat-

and began again in unison with hers.

It wasn't the words he said that won her heart,

but the quiet assurance she felt.

G.C. Bailey

She heightened his senses

and numbed his pain.

My heart waited for her

even long after it was foolish to do so.

Burnt By The Sun

She was the sun
And I, the sun worshiper.
"Fly high to her warmth!"
Said I, full of love.

I made my plans
And constructed wings
Made of glue and feathers,
That I might fly to my love.

But as I flew,
Reaching heights where only eagles soar,
The sun bore down upon me-
My glue and feathers became undone.

And like Icarus, the Greek of old,
I fell twenty thousand feet
Downward back towards earth.
My life and plans brought to naught.

Alas, I have been burnt by the sun.

Though it may bring much pain,

it is folly to have never fully loved.

G.C. Bailey

We communicate with understanding

though no word is uttered;

for we listen from within,

and speak from our hearts.

Of The Sea

My arms ache to hold her.

My eyes ache to see her.

My ears ache to hear her.

My lips ache to kiss her.

My heart dies to love her.

G.C. Bailey

She spoke though no word was said;

for I was listening to her with my heart.

Go To Sleep

Go to sleep,
Morning is nigh.
My watch says
It's two forty-five.

Rest your head,
Don't you cry.
And I will sing
A lullaby.

Soon my love,
I'll have to go.
When I'll be back,
I don't know.

But rest your head,
It will be ok.
I'll think of you
Every day.

Go to sleep,
Please close your eyes.
You shouldn't see
Me start to cry.

When I'm gone,
Please remember me.
Know I love you
So tenderly.

May I have
A gentle kiss?
Just a small one
You won't miss.

Now go to sleep,
It's getting late.
I'll be gone
When you awake.

Don't you worry,
I'll write soon.
And every night
I'll dream of you.

My love for her is insatiable;

my desire consumes me;

my lonely heart destroys me.

True love is as deep and boundless as the sea.

Drink of it until you can consume no more…

and drown in it.

Of The Sea

For me,

    love alone

        is proof enough

            that God exists.

Many were vexed that I had no sense to quit her,

but I did not possess

the ability,

nor the desire,

to cease loving her.

The only void greater than the heavens

is the one that is in my heart.

Those who say there is no God are fools.

For how can one look into the eyes of the woman he loves

and not believe that only a divine being

could create such a perfect creature?

Final Wish

One hundred feet left to go
The young soldier whispered in his head,
But as the rockets began to explode
He knew he would soon be dead.

One hundred feet left to go,
As shrapnel and death ripped by
Knocking the soldier off his feet
As he rose, a vision he did spy:

He saw his father, his mother, his sisters, and
brothers
All this did enter his mind,
And when he saw his true love's face
The soldier shouted out and cried:

"Lord please help me,
Please allow me, my love once more to see!
I've never asked you once for a favor,
But now I beg you upon bended knee!"

One hundred feet left to go
The young soldier got up and ran
And found the safety of the bunker
His life saved by God's merciful hand.

One hundred feet now left behind
The soldier again knelt and prayed.
Thanking the Lord for sparing his life
And granting him another day.

Seven thousand miles now left behind,
The war over and done.
The soldier came home and found his love,
And thanked God for making him the lucky one.

G.C. Bailey

The Hunter

I feel the hair on my neck stiffen
In the cool November breeze.
I sniff the air and catch the scent
Of earth and pine trees.
I sense my quarry;
Sitting silent and quite frightened;
My nerves become edgy,
As all my senses are heightened.

My muscles quiver,
Afraid to upset the delicate balance.
I am trained;
My muscles are strong and my feet calloused.
I stand rigid as only my eyes move
In search of the prey,
I want to attack,
But I have my orders that I must obey.

My best friend approaches
With weapon in his hand;
He excels as a companion;
I've known no better man.
I hold my position
And show him where the quarry lies,
My companion steps forward

Of The Sea

To their hiding place and pries.

I see the game tremble then stiffen,
Preparing to take flight,
When I coil and jump at them
With all of my might.
There's a rustle, a bustle,
A flurry, and flush,
And up come four quail
Beating their wings with a rush.

Out of the bushes,
They spring at breakneck speed.
My companion pulls his shotgun
And quickly draws a bead.
He squeezes the trigger;
Making an expert shot.
I follow the bird down,
Then rush to its spot.

I lean down and take
The downed bird in my jaw,
When I hear my friend,
My name loudly call.
I quickly return
And proudly show him the catch;

G.C. Bailey

We are the perfect team-
There is no better match.

My friend pats my head
And tells me to "hunt on."
In a flash to find other birds-
I am gone.
Of all the hunting dogs
There is none better,
Oh, how I love my life
As an English Setter!

A fine shotgun is like a beautiful woman;

Curvaceous, potentially deadly, and expensive…

But a shotgun will never break your heart.

Words can take a life or they can renew a broken soul.

Choose your words wisely.

Of The Sea

Women often settle for males

Who don't put forth any effort.

A man will work to earn a woman's trust, respect, and love.

If he won't work to earn you, he isn't worth it.

The difference between a boy, a man, and a male,

is easily discernible.

Of The Sea

He reached for her hand and she readily gave it.

After all those years, their bodies had aged

But their love was as strong and full of youth

As though it was their first day together.

Parenthood is watching your child grow,

seeing the same strengths and weaknesses you possess;

and praying he won't bear the same scars

that you carry on his behalf.

Shine Brighter Than The Stars

1. Tonight the moon
Shines in splendid grace.
Moonbeams dance
Upon thy radiant face.

2. Billions of stars
Twinkle so bright,
Vying for thy attention
With their flickering lights.

3. Thou art also a constellation
In my heart burning bright.
There thou art cherished
By both day and night.

4. And thy light guides me
No matter how near or far.

And I shall always find thee- for you

Shine brighter than the stars.

Her heart was like a shattered glass vase.
And each time her heart was broken,
Upon the shards she cut herself.

But he loved her and endured every painful cut
And through the painful cuts and tears,
He glued her pieces back together.

Of The Sea

It was there, in the midst of his darkest hour,
That he heard her voice,
And he gained the courage to carry on.

His hands, now old, wrinkled and shaky from the years, held her head.

But when she looked up into his eyes,

She still saw the same youthful sparkle that had always been.

The Toiling Heart

My heart toils, toils, toils, without rest.

Yearning for her, it beats at my chest.

Day and night it cries for its soulmate.

The pain from longing is unbearably great.

But suddenly it stops beating at all,

And I know that all of me will fall.

Softly it begins beating once again,

Yet now there is peace from within.

For my hearts search has come to an end,

Because it led me back to you, my best friend.

For Stan

Beware the Ides of March,
That wretched day!
When the cancer came
And took my best friend away.

Too young to have died,
Too soon a death.
Yet you remained strong,
Even 'til your last breath.

I was away hundreds of miles
When I heard the news.
My head hung low,
My cries over losing you were profuse.

The day of your funeral,
I could not attend.
My sadness turned bitter,
As do hearts on the mend.

It was a full year
Before I made it out to the place
Where quietly you lay,
In peaceful grace.

And there we cried;
Those who loved you most,
As we poured two fingers of bourbon
And gave a final toast.

A final farewell
To the man who walked among men:
"Rest in peace our dear brother and dear friend,
'Til we meet again in heaven."

The hardest part about loving thee

Was that thou didst love indifferently.

I find my soul refreshed,
when quail hunting among southern pines,
with a good dog, a fine shotgun, and men I respect.

Of The Sea

I took her head in my hands,
Her hair between my fingers dancing.

I looked deep into her eyes,
Saw her anticipating.

I pulled her close;
Both our hearts racing.

And I kissed her hard.

They cried from laughing

As they remembered the good times together,

And cried from sadness,

Because they knew those times were gone.

An Untamable Soul

She wanted me to be a businessman;

Polished, well dressed, and a socialite

Living amongst a sea of skyscrapers and people.

But I bore a wild heart and untamable soul.

I belonged in the wilderness by campfires,

Under the stars, drinking bourbon,

And chasing intangible dreams.

It's when she says she's at her worst-

Her hair is wild and unkempt,

Or she simply dons shorts and a t-shirt,

Or she hasn't put on her makeup.

But that is when I see her divine mess,

And I can't stop staring-

And I fall in love all over again.

My Country 'Tis For Thee

My country 'tis for thee

That friends died valiantly

So we may always be free.

Land that they loved so dear

The call to duty did hear

To save the oppressed far and near

And serve thy people with cheer.

One nation under God may we

Unite and remembering

The toils our fathers made for thee

That freedom may ring.

From the mountains of Alaska

To the plains of Oklahoma

And to my sweet coastal Georgia

May we unite as one for our country-
America!

Of The Sea

Both loved the other too much,

To risk saying what desire

Was burning in their hearts.

So, they suffered the same pain together-alone.

G.C. Bailey

Women who say men don't cry have never seen a
man's lifelong dream realized or destroyed-
Nor seen a man with a broken heart.

She was everything to him.
She was poetry in motion.
She spilled onto the pages of his heart.

G.C. Bailey

A Great Depression

How often have I seen you with these bouts,
As you struggle through anxiety and doubts?
Debilitated, unable to clearly think and do.
Exhausted to the point that you're unable to
move.

Circle patterns in your catastrophic thoughts,
Only bring your joy to naught.
Your downward spirals are dangerous too,
And lead to a deep depression within you.

And we who love you suffer too,
Not knowing how to help, or what to say or do.
We suffer with you and cry from within
When we see your happiness quickly expend.

To break these patterns I'll do all what I must,
To make you smile and earn your trust.
You simply don't know what it does to me
To see you sad and so unhappy.

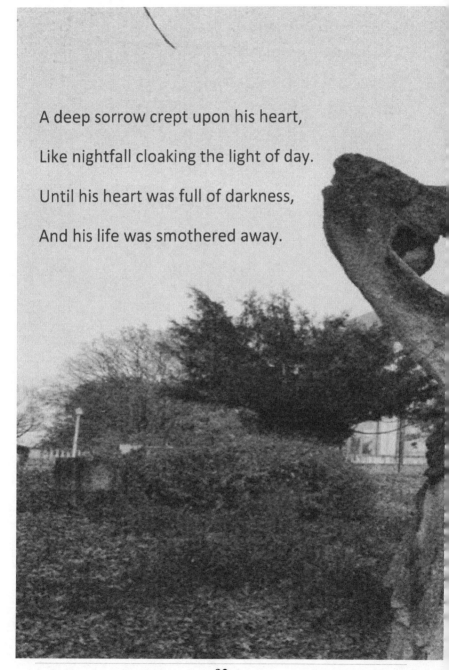

A deep sorrow crept upon his heart,

Like nightfall cloaking the light of day.

Until his heart was full of darkness,

And his life was smothered away.

When I first saw you it took my breath.
When I heard your laugh it took my heart.
When I fell in love it took all of me.

G.C. Bailey

Sometimes love means dying to yourself

to the point that you are willing to let them go,

so that they can be happy.

Of The Sea

Protect her heart

And one day she will show you

how high she can fly.

Of The Sea

One should not measure a relationship

by the lack of conflicts,

but how those conflicts are resolved.

G.C. Bailey

A Soldier's Suicide

I once knew a young soldier- nearly a boy
Who followed his orders with a heart full of joy.
He went to war and saw things no man should.
He made the best of it and did all he could.

But demons found him that he couldn't shake,
Until their presence he could no longer take.
And one dark night in pouring rain,
He took his rifle and blew out his brain.

They sent his body home to be laid to rest,
Then went about their duties with heavy chests.
I pray that you all may never know
The hell where these young men go.

Loving you was never a mistake.

It was my highest honor.

She goes here and there, undeterred and unalarmed.

She is protected.

For I sit and watch over her;

Ready to impart violence on her behalf.

A Lovers Song

We were as in love as lovers could be,
I for her and she for me,
Long summers spent under the old oak tree.
Cuddled together and talking sweetly.

We knew we were meant to be,
I with her and she with me,
And our dreams blossomed and we began to see
Our lives together growing old peacefully.

But one summer ended too soon and I had to leave,
For enlistment into the US Army.
Love's pangs thrashed between her and me,
Yet still we dreamed of what we believed would
be.

We knew we were meant to be,
I with her and she with me
I wrote her everyday from Basic Training,
And signed every letter *Tenderly*.

Finally, one day I was granted leave.
I told her to go under the old oak tree.
I met my love and upon one knee
I asked my love to marry me.

G.C. Bailey

Now we are married,
I to her and she to me.
We live together in love and harmony
And our children play on the old oak tree.

In the end, I found myself back at the very beginning.

Back to the place where it all started - with you.

He had written many a correspondence letter,
Usually closing with *Sincerely* or *Best Regards*.
But there was one valediction-
One word that he reserved for only letters to her;
Letters he signed simply *Tenderly*.

Death of a Captain

1. Under the crescent moon
   By the thrashing sea,
   I lay gasping for breath
   Upon the glistening beach.

2. Somewhere in the distance
   Across the waters black abyss
   I could hear the beams breaking
   As my ship dashed upon the cliffs.

3. How many souls lost this night?
   Cried I, from within my soul.
   Trying to rise, exhaustion overtook me.
   Back, back I fell, into the shoal.

4. Morning came and went
   With the sun high I finally woke,
   And scattered round I saw my fellow sailors.
   It was then a faint voice spoke.

5. "All is lost, none are left
   All those brave souls swallowed by the sea,
   Despair now foolish Captain
   For all that's left is you and me!

6. Hopelessly stranded on this desert isle
   Brought to ruin by thy greed,
   I curse the day I ever knew you
   And embarked upon the cursed sea!"

7. Then a pistol he raised,
   Leveled upon my chest,
   I saw the flash and felt the ball
   Enter deep into my breast.

8. The earth was spinning round and round.
   I reeled and fell upon the ground.
   Killed in search of fortune and fame,
   Nevermore to see my homeland again.

I would rather my hands be calloused,

My body boned tired, and caked in dirt and sweat,

But bear a happy heart,

Than be comfortable with a soul,

That slowly decayed from within.

My Roots Are Buried Here

I have travelled the world
And visited faraway places
I have seen mountains, forests, and deserts
And passed all types of faces.

But there is nothing in this world
My heart could ever want more
Than to smell the sweet pines
That make my soul soar.

To be home in Georgia
That's where I long to dwell.
Perhaps one day I will return
Then once more my heart will be well.

My sweet Georgia;
May my song always be
"mis raices estan aqui."

Kiss Me Now

Kiss me now my dear,
We've already wasted so much time,
Kiss me now my dear,
And I shall make you mine.

Kiss me now my dear,
Our beating hearts do wait,
Kiss me now my dear
There's nothing left to anticipate.

Kiss me now my dear,
For you belong with me,
Kiss me now my dear,
And I will love you through eternity.

I don't know when I first realized that I loved you;

I just know that I did.

Of The Sea

I see the storms billowing behind your eyes.

You say everything is fine but you're telling me lies.

If only I had a way to prove

He'll never be the right man for you.

A Beautiful War

We were at an impasse: our wills were not the same.
And when politics and reasoning failed,
We began a protracted war.

And what a beautiful war it was.
She was more cunning than I,
For when I fired a barrage of words she would retreat
And I thought that battle won.

Instead, she created an insurgency and waited
Until long after I had forgotten the battle,
And she would strike with ferocity.

But in the end, we loved another.
And when our resources for fighting,
And energy had been depleted,
We went back and made peace.

And that was even more beautiful than the war.

I loved her *wildly*.

I was unbridled and full of hope.

Even now, *I love her still.*

G.C. Bailey

She looks at me and I become unraveled.
She sees to my soul and knows my thoughts
are all dependent upon one constant- her.

Of The Sea

Even though we're apart, you and I

View the same stars, under the same sky.

And no matter where we are or where we lie,

Those same stars for us will shine.

G.C. Bailey

I only wish to brush your hair behind your ear,
Kiss your forehead, and tell you I love you.

A Lifetime Ago

I only wanted to be as one

Loving her from dusk to dawn

I bore ideals that were innocent and true

When we were young and love was new.

I never could have known

A broken heart was inevitable

To earn my way I'd have to pay

And bear my soul each and every day.

I walk the streets at night alone

Wondering where did I go wrong

Her memories racing through my mind

And all I can do is sit alone and cry.

I know I'm not the only one

To bear an unrequited love

Yet still the pain within me seethes

It hurts to the point that I can hardly breathe.

G.C. Bailey

I wish I could forget my broken heart

Make a new life, make a new start

But my heart won't set her free

And I wonder if she thinks of me.

I miss her laugh, I miss her scent

I miss our talks, I miss my best friend

Life seemed so simple and under our control

But now that seems like a lifetime ago.

WHEN A WOMAN COMPLIMENTS A MAN,

ALL HIS BARRIERS ARE SHATTERED,

AND HE IS ABSOLUTELY DISARMED.

You are the rarest of flowers

And I, but a lowly gardener.

But I will tenderly cultivate our relationship,

And you will blossom for me.

Of The Sea

He had fought in two wars;

his heart was scarred and heavy.

But losing her wounded him

in ways that war never could.

The Protector

From health and safety
I turned to your cries,
And flew to you
Through the darkening skies.
Night could not delay,
Nor danger keep me away.
I heard your desperate plea
And sped to my friend in need.

I came to your side
In a fiery rage,
And fought to keep
Your demons at bay.
Should danger again come to your door,
I'll answer your call, just as before.
Even though I am far away,
I heard you, I loved you, and came.

The seasons of life are ever changing.

Like a river, we ebb and flow.

In our spring, we laughed and our love flowed.

In summer, our fiery passions showed.

Fall fell upon us and your heart became cold.

By winter, my only companion was my shadow.

I anxiously await spring again.

For I miss happy times with my best friend.

Being a man of my word,
I kept my promise.

At the cost of a grieving heart.

Of The Sea

Storms and rains rampage upon your life,
But the sun will soon shine upon you again.

Above the clouds there is always a clear sky.

G.C. Bailey

The Ballad of Robert McCrae

High and alone in the machan,
Sat the brave Robert McCrae,
Watching the brush below,
Where the body of a young girl now lay.
Not twelve years of age, the poor girl half eaten,
Having become a leopard's prey.

That poor girl,
Snatched from the field in mid-day,
By the very leopard that had terrified
Every poor village in the valley.
It was not a leopard but an evil spirit,
Robert had heard the villagers say.

Light was fading fast.
Shadows turned the green leaves to gray.
Darkness crept upon the tree,
Where sat Robert McCrae.
Gazing into darkness,
He waited for the leopard to return to his prey.

Suddenly, everything was amplified;
His heartbeat pounded his ears.
Robert scanned the jungle floor;
He knew the leopard was near.
For the silence of the jungle
Made the leopard's presence clear.

The sound of crunching bones,
Then a shadow appeared darker than the rest.
McCrae stiffened further.
His heart was pumping and thumping in his chest.
Slowly, his fingers searched for the safety
Of his 400 Nitro Express.

Of The Sea

He could hear the tearing of flesh
And the leopard licking his chops.
McCrae felt the cold ridge of the safety
And slowly switched it off.
The safety made a click.
The leopard abruptly stopped.

Gazing intently, he no longer saw
The shadow upon the ground.
Cautiously and ever so slowly,
McCrae looked around.
The leopard had climbed the tree above
And now was looking down.

The great cat sprang,
With a terrifying growl
McRae turned the rifle,
Firing both barrel's rounds.
He heard the bullet strike its mark
As the leopard fell to the ground.

It was late at night.
His body tired and sore,
McRae to the villagers,
The leopard's body bore.
The leopard brought to ruin
To terrify no more.

McRae gently lay the leopard
Upon the ground for all to see.
Oh what celebration!
Oh what jubilee!
"McCrae has killed the maneater!"
They cried triumphantly.

G.C. Bailey

Once you find her,   .
Your heart will let you know.
That she is the one for you,
And to never let her go.

There by the stream I find myself again.

And there I dream of her...

and of what might have been.

Addition

Heroin, OxyContin, Cocaine, and Weed,

Prescription pills, Methamphetamines, and PCP.

All the drugs that people use

To make themselves feel happy and loose.

And I too have long been addicted

To that which makes my heart less afflicted.

Syringes, Pipes, glasses of Booze,

Nothing is required for the drug I use.

My high is natural, starting at the heart,

And overtakes my sense with a quick start.

Huffing, Shooting, Snorting, and Sniffing glue,

I don't need all that. My addiction is you.

You are a delicate flower;

I shall tend your every need.

You blossomed into a garden within my heart,

And there you shall remain eternally.

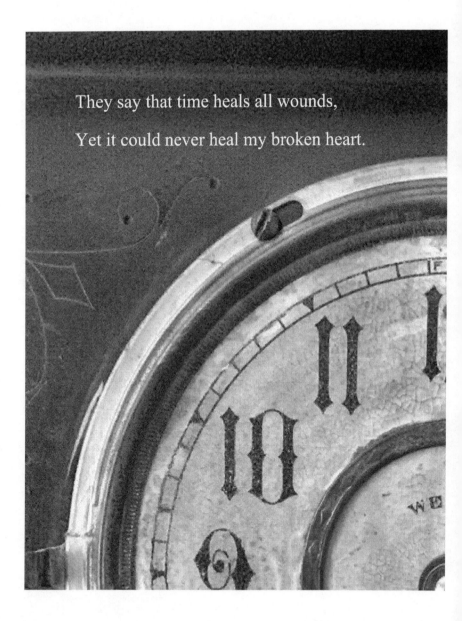

They say that time heals all wounds,

Yet it could never heal my broken heart.

Of The Sea

Even in the endless dark
She shines like a beacon upon my heart.

She is not Helen of Troy.

Her face did not launch ten thousand ships.

Nor is she like a muse.

Her sweet voice did not run sailors aground.

But she launched a fleet within my heart

And her voice gave my soul wings.

End of Watch

You answered the call that few men hear.
You laid aside your insecurity and fear.
You began a whole new career,
And joined the thin blue line.

Training was tough and at times made you cry,
But you wouldn't let others down and so continued to try.
You knew out there that it meant to live or die,
And you loved the thin blue line.

Like a sheepdog protecting the herd,
You stood ready to protect and serve.
You remained humble, professional, and reserved,
And you honored the thin blue line.

You gave an oath to your badge and "the public trust"
And were ready and willing to die if you must,
To protect those who were treated unjust,
And you fought for the thin blue line.

Now roll call is made for "Badge 2-1-4!"
But there is no answer anymore.
A bugle sounds as a multitude mourns,
Standing by a grave that flowers adorn.
You did your duty
And held the thin blue line,
Sleep well dear brother; this watch is mine.

She didn't know where he was going,
Or if it was even safe.
But she knew that he'd find an adventure-
And that she would share it with him.

Of The Sea

The Virus

I lay on the white hospital bed,
Doctors and nurses all round my head.
For my condition there is no cure,
It was a viral infection, of that they were sure.
I lay there writhing in pain without hope.
My throat was parched and my airway choked.
Others down the hall heard my shrill cries
And marveled how I was even still alive.
Finally, one morning a nurse found me upon the floor;
My soul had departed, my body would know pain no more.
They said I had contracted COVID-19 from the start,
But the virus which tormented me was love-
I died from a broken heart.

LOVE

Lost in her words and

Overcome with emotion,

Vibrating within my soul is

Everlasting devotion.

It's always the same as it was at the start;
I'm left alone with a broken heart.

G.C. Bailey

My heart was a barren and frozen tundra,

As uninhabitable as the Bering Strait.

You are the single Delicate

That blossomed in the desolation.

You gave beauty to my bleak world,

And breathed life into my soul.

143

The End

Nothing will erase this deep sadness
That I continually feel.
I have bore it so long
That it seems surreal.

I sit alone and coming undone;
Living has become a chore.
I can no longer go on like this.
I feel the cold steel of the thirty-eight bore.

This isn't how I wanted it to end
But know no other way,
To bear this sadness any longer,
I cannot endure another day.

I left you a note telling you that I'm truly sorry
But I can't live with so much pain,
And ask that you'll forgive me one last time
For placing this pistol to my brain.

As long as you remain in my heart,
I will always be home.

Of The Sea

They walked together, hand in hand,

But they were holding each other's hearts.

Broken

I stood like a rock
Against the world's rages and fears.
I waded through the toils
With blood, sweat, and tears.

But there was one thing
That made my heart weak,
And it was the thought of her;
Beautiful and meek.

Love hit me like a wave.
I buckled and fell.
I picked myself back up again,
How many times, I'll never tell.

And through loves emotions,
I struggled relentlessly.
But in the end I came undone,
When she
completely,
utterly,
broke me.

G.C. Bailey

That Boy, This Boy

That boy is no good for you,
He won't be true.
Deep down you know it too.
That boy will only break your heart.

This boy loves you so
That it hurts to let you go.
In your heart I think you know
This boy will only love you.

That boy will only make you cry,
But for you I would die.
If you'd just give me some time,
I will make you mine.

As we lie between the sheets,

Laughing, loving in warm embrace.

I gaze upon your radiant face

Beautiful- full of beauty and grace.

And I wonder how you could you ever love me,

Then you say "this is how we were meant to be."

In one kiss

You will know.

All the things I left unsaid.

For Her

A thousand times in my head I say her name.
I love her and will never be the same.

Before her Armani perfume fills the air,
Before I see her flowing hair,

Before I see her beauty that forces my stare,
I feel her presence and my heart is ensnared.

When she smiles all the clouds roll away.
When she laughs night turns to day.

When she touches my hand my heart grows weak.
When she enters the room I am unable to speak.

She changed me into better man
For her I'll do everything I can.

Suddenly, I saw all my hopes and dreams wrecked;
Like a vessel dashed upon the rocks.
Together we sank beneath life's cruel and icy seas.

Of The Sea

If toxic masculinity means pursuing her relentlessly,

Showing her that she is the most important thing in my life,

And protecting her femininity with every fiber of my being,

Then I shall relish the title.

When I came home,

You made it feel as though I never left.

Only then did the deep wounds in my heart,

Left over from the war,

Begin to heal

I bear a wild and tumultuous soul.

I write to calm my own spirit.

To make pain somehow palatable.

If others enjoy my words,

I hope the words move their soul.

That they may reach new heights,

to a place unknown before.

Til There Was You

I never knew how sweet a voice could sound.

I never knew there was such beauty all around.

I didn't know a heart could hurt so.

Nor did I know how much a heart could grow.

I never knew what it meant to cry.

I didn't know love hurt so, you wished to die.

I didn't know how much ignorance is bliss.

I didn't know all you could say with a kiss.

I didn't know how happy I could be.

There was so much I didn't see.

'Til there was you.

I would rather die at the hands of my friend

Than in the arms of my enemy.

Rough Men

Rough men stand ready to pay the ultimate price.

To keep people safe, they make great sacrifice.

Working through birthdays and holidays too,

They do not rest until the mission is through.

These hardened men will always answer the call,

To maintain peace, order, and security for us all.

Time has made me older,

But loving you kept my heart young.

EVERY NIGHT
I FALL ASLEEP SAYING YOUR NAME.

EVERY DAY
I AWAKE CRYING IT OUT AGAIN.

The Searchers

You don't know what you want,
So I'm asking
If you need a hand.
I'll be there for you,
So just ask me,
I'll help you in any way I can.

You're trying to find
Your place in this world.
I can't imagine how hard it must be
For a dreaming girl.

But when you find
Everything you're looking for,
I hope that life
Leads you to my front door.

I know what I want,
It's the not having
The thing that I want most.
The tyranny of distance
Is distracting,
And keeping me from pulling you close.

G.C. Bailey

I'm like you, trying to find my way
But everyone I meet, in every new place,
Tells me I should be with you
And waking up to your face.

And when I've found
Everything that I looked for,
I know that life
Will lead me back to your front door.

But if it won't,
I'll keep searching for you.
And I hope that you'll keep searching too
And I'll know my search is through
When I come home and find you.

We judge others by their actions.

We judge ourselves by our intentions.

G.C. Bailey

I would walk a million miles

To give her all that she needs.

I would walk a million more

Simply to die at her feet.

Home is where the heart is,
And I am homesick for you.

A man will become inpatient and angry

When he sees life passing him by,

And unfulfilled dreams still dwell in his breast.

The Pistolero

1. He lost his love in the springtime,
   His wife and child now dead.
   He rode out early one morning,
   And swore he'd never return again.

2. He rode all through the night,
   And all through the next day,
   But he could never ride far enough
   To make her memory fade.

3. He found himself by the river
   That borders Old Mexico,
   And decided he'd make a living
   As an outlaw Pistolero.

4. He joined a band of outlaws,
   Their names were known quite well.
   They robbed, rustled, and murdered
   He knew he'd join them in hell.

5. He was driven by the loss of his woman.
   She visited him in his dreams.
   His sorrow pushed him onward,
   And led him to terrible deeds.

6. One night he was stopped by the sheriff
   While robbing the bank in town.
   He drew his six gun and fired,
   And gunned the poor sheriff down.

7. They placed a reward for five thousand pesos,
    Five thousand pesos they placed on his head.
    To catch the Pistolero-
    Alive or maybe dead.

8. The posse caught him in the canyon.
    Surrounded, he made his last stand.
    The Pistolero was fast as lightning
    And filled three full of lead.

9. They fired down from all sides.
    He felt a bullet go deep in his chest.
    "My dear Maria I'm coming"
    Were his words as he took his final breath.

10. Sometimes in the desert at night,
    When a soft and cool wind blows,
    You can hear the sound of laughter.
    It's the laugh of Maria and her dear Pistolero.

We sat on the runway gazing at the stars,

And listened to the passing distant cars.

We watched the moon and constellations.

She spoke of her dreams and consternations.

But when she asked of my dreams in turn,

My only dream had been to be there with her.

G.C. Bailey

My Hometown

All by myself,

With this great big world before me,

But it's not for me, it's for someone else.

I've tried and tried again,

To let you know just where my heart is,

To tell the truth and not pretend.

All I had to do was get away,

Only to realize I was meant to stay.

Where the hawk flies high over planted fields,

Where time slows down and there's gentle people,

In my hometown, my hometown.

I thought I made it clear, do I have to say it?

I've always loved you, you just didn't see it,

All I need is you and me and my home.

I'm coming back, I'm coming back.

Soon you'll see, you were meant for me.

I'm coming back-to you.

Of The Sea

I wanted to stay
But my broken heart wouldn't let me
And so I sought riches and fame
And I left, it's true,
But now I know I could never be happy
Unless I am with you

Where I hear your laugh in the whispering pines,
Where the whippoorwill sings his proud song at night,
In my hometown, my hometown.
Where the stars at night surpass all others,
Where you and I first became lovers,
In my hometown, my hometown.

I'm coming back, I'm coming back.
Soon you'll see, you were meant for me.
I'm coming back-to you.

She is a goddess.

Of divine contradictions.

May this epitaph upon my gravestone be read:
The tragedy of his life was not his death,
But that he longed for her until his final breath.

G.C. Bailey

Of The Sea

Like Venus, born from the sea,
This too is how she came to be;
Rising from a shell swept onto the beach.
No words can describe such a creation of beauty.

With eyes of the deepest hue,
Lips soft as the morning dew,
And skin lightly kissed by the sun.
Oh! But she is a marvel to look upon.

A goddess walks amongst us mere mortal men,
Who are unworthy to even touch her garment hem.
And I, the most unworthy of them all,
Fell in love when her beauty saw.

But unlike others, I saw her beauty from within,
And my desire for her was not a sin.
Mine eyes are not worthy to look upon that face
That shines so brightly in beauty and grace.

She calmed the storms that within me raged.
Her gentle voice banished my swells of fear away.
Where once was a dark and shallow shoal,
Waves of love now overflow.

G.C. Bailey

She calms the waters, they now softly roll.
She shines like a beacon within my soul.
I'll serve my goddess' every need
With only humble and tender deeds.

Upon my lips I call her sweet name,
Awaiting the arrival of my queen again.
Oh, blessed be that wondrous day,
When out of the sea she came!

About the Author

Author G.C. Bailey is a US Army Field Artillery officer and veteran. His immersion in the profession of arms and lifelong passion for poetry and short stories lend an unparalleled authenticity to experiences in life; including love, loss, and combat. G.C. Bailey is a native of Statesboro, GA currently living in Oklahoma. He is an avid outdoorsman and spends most of his free time hunting, fishing, exploring, and writing. New to the writing field, his current writing has consisted a reflective hunting story for "Sporting Dog Journal"

Made in the USA
Columbia, SC
07 March 2023